THE FIFTEENTH
FLOWER

SARAH PINGEL

Disclaimer: This book portrays struggles with mental health and contains graphic wording.

Edited by Taelor Monkman DeWeese

ISBN: 979-8-9910214-0-1

Also available as an eBook

This book is not just for me or my journey, but for the people who share the same pains and the same strength to heal. I hope this book finds you and helps you feel seen.

Aster

Like autumn leaves falling from a dying tree, my soul fell from my body. My heavy heart did not palpitate like the heart of a girl who smiled authentically every day. It beat out of the chest of a girl who had tears streaming off her cheeks and seeping into the crevice of her chest. My family wrote off my pain as yesterday's news and cackled as if wanting to kill myself was a funny joke —it could never actually happen. My friends laughed in their responses, saying, "Me too," as if they did not hear me begging for help —as if I was just nervous about a math test or complaining about a boy not texting me back. Life felt helpless, as if no matter how hard I cried, no one could hear me. I want to lay in a downpour and wait for the pounding droplets to drown me.

Couldn't anybody stop to help me?

Couldn't anyone hear me screaming for them?

No one seems to notice that I am dying. Maybe they do, maybe they don't care. It wouldn't matter if a single soul cared anyway. In this mind of mine, the agony eats away at the joy. It devours the hope that someone will save me, that someone will hold me. I drift in a sea of unaccompanied sorrow, my brown hair wet and mangy as it sinks beneath the surface of my floating body. My mind is so muddled with grief that my heart is beginning to bleed black. Like poison dripping down my organs, my stupid body is failing to survive.

Sometimes, I think about my family and how I wish they could help me, but I've never really considered them… helpful. My sisters have their own lives to deal with, so they don't really care about their little sisters' problems. My dad is busy, too, but I wouldn't confide in him anyway. He always brushes off the idea of mental health, so he is not the best person to talk to about the demise of my brain. My mom tries to be there for me, but her compassion doesn't shine through the way she thinks it does. I feel like I'm floating beneath the rest of my family, gliding across the floor, trying to watch out for their feet. I think it hurts worse waiting to be crushed than the actual crushing.

I wish they'd just step on me already.

The sun seemed to wake me every morning with what others would call a *bright glimmer* coming through my window. To me, though, it just looked *gray*. Drab and gloomy, as if clouds decided to creep into my bedroom to push out the sunshine, blocking out any possibility of joy. My feet drag as they swing off my bed, and slowly, yet surely, I finally stand up. In the mornings, leaving the safety of my covers is hard. They smelled like my mom's vanilla candles mixed with the natural sweet scent of my skin.

I just want to lay in bed and suffocate.

I slip on a dress from my closet that runs down my legs and blends its white cotton with my fluorescent skin. Walking to the vanity beside my warm bed, I look through the small mirror to tame my wild hair before finally walking out my door. Seeping into my living room, the smell of my mom's hot spearmint tea infused the air. Her reading glasses sit beside her while she pats her face with makeup. She always wears a foundation-covered headband to keep the strands of her blonde hair tucked away from the debris.

"Look who's finally up," she scoffs as she checks the clock to see it is past noon. She goes back to applying her mascara before giving me a chance to respond. Giving a quick smile to the side of her head, I continue walking towards the front door.

I just want to die.

I wish she'd see that through my fake ass smile.

Childlike footprints imprint under me with each step I take. Too young to be taken seriously, apparently too old to ask for help. My bony body and moonlight skin starkly contrast with the lively, warm sun, soaking up as much vitamin D as possible. I plan for death often, so I try to enjoy the little things, such as the dew left on the grass after it's rained or the way rocks sparkle if you hold them in the light. I think about how flowers bloom bigger when they're being nourished and how I, too, wish to be nourished. I wish to be held, fed, and cared for gently so I can bloom like the flower buds surrounding me — growing to my best potential. Instead, my petals wither, and my stem peels as I begin to die underneath the dirt.

Dizzy in my thoughts, I walk upon a tree, big enough to block the free, undisturbed, clear blue sky above it. I had been walking for a while now, trying to escape the thoughts of my expiration.

"Hello." Startled, I look around the tree's branches. Is it talking to me? Am I imagining a voice amid my loneliness? I decide to ignore it, whether it be a real voice or my own head.

"Hello?" The voice says again, a nasal chirp erupting when it speaks. I look back into the tree's leaves, getting out of my brain and back into reality. I suppose I should answer; if it really is someone talking to me, I shouldn't be rude.

"Hello?" I finally answer, looking around to see the person attached to the voice. No one answered, but a young girl walked around the tree trunk, stopping only five feet from me. Her baby fat still sat in her rosy cheeks; her body was tiny for her age, or from what I guessed her age was. She wore a white dress just like mine that flowed around her ankles whenever a gust was in the wind.

"Hi," she says, looking up at me. Her eyes a deep blue, her skin pale, her hair brown with a hint of fire in the sunlight. She looks so familiar, like staring back at myself in a mirror.

"H-hello," I say, repetitively striking my tied tongue once again.

"Are you lost?" she asks. The question was simple enough, but still, I had to think. Physically speaking, I am not. Mentally speaking, I am.

"In a way, yes." I finally mutter quietly.

"Can I help?"

"Probably not," she pauses for a second, taking in my response. I look from her and back to my bare feet as they sit in the dirt, blood draining from my face and welling up in my toes as I wait for this figment of my imagination to say something back to me.

"Can I try?" she asked, breaking the silence we were floating in. Finally, lifting my head to look back at her with a slight smile, I utter one word,

"Sure."

Welcome to the world
of an unheard whisper.

Welcome - Sarah Pingel

Anxiety

The girl looked upon me like I would disappear if she looked away for even a second. We stood still for what felt like hours.

Sure.

Why did I say sure? I don't need this little girl's help. I'm used to being alone, why did I accept her invitation so fast? Why is she looking at me like that? Why does she look so familiar? My heart pounds in my chest as it crushes within itself. Why am I accepting her help? No one ever wants to help me, and now some strange-familiar-small girl does? Why? She continues to watch me, not a single expression crossing her face until I sit on the ground beside her.

Thoughts fill my whole body. I feel how I do when I have to go in public and speak to other human beings with the possibility of them thinking I'm annoying. Everyone gets sick of me eventually; in reality, though, I believe they're sick of me right away; they just don't want to admit it because lying to my face is somehow better than hurting my feelings. Either way, I'm a nuisance to others, and now I will be a bother to this poor-simular-tiny girl when I don't even know why I agreed for her to help me with my lost soul in the first place.

I'm so irritating.

"Jane?" I hear the teensy voice say. The fog begins to lift from my eyes and thin in my head. The strange girl is kneeling next to me, her light brown brows pinched into a worried state. Her petite hand is placed on my hand as it clutches the grass below me.

"Are you okay?" she asks, her voice slightly breaking. I nod because words can't seem to leave my mouth. She smiles as she wraps her hand into mine so that she's what I'm holding instead of the grass beneath me.

"Panic attacks are scary," she claims lightly. "But it's going to be okay. The storm will pass, and you'll be able to stand again." I watch her speak as the fog in my head becomes mere mist.

"I know you feel you're a burden, but you're not. I want to sit beside you, and I want to hold your hand. As much as it feels like people are against you and it makes your heart squeeze, I will stay beside you whenever you need the sun to shine through the clouds." She soothed as her sweet smile grew from cheek to cheek, and her eyes lit with love. My heart calms to its normal rhythm as a smile slightly crosses my face. It is much smaller than hers by a long shot, yet she somehow smiles bigger when she sees mine.

After a moment of silence, the girl with the dark blue eyes stands up and pulls me up with her. I stand and wipe the dust off my lace as she does the same, mirroring me in actions as she already does in appearance.

"Should we start looking for what you lost?" she asks as she walks a bit ahead of the tree that still stood above us. I look back down the hill that I trudged up to meet this tree and this girl; then I look back at the direction she was looking in.

"Let's go," I reply as determination crosses my eyeline. She beams with light again before we both head toward the missing piece of my mind.

I wish I could live in a tree:

Making tea in my kettle,

as I feel the warmth inside nature.

I could live inside the bark as the tree teaches me how to

grow.

I would grow strong,

and my mind would be green.

By myself,

where no one could make me feel like I'm suffocating.

I Want to Thrive Outside - Sarah Pingel

I feel my face flush

as my vision becomes blurry.

My breaths are short,

my lungs are aching.

My body is shaking fiercely.

I want it to stop.

I feel like my body is shutting down.

The walls around me are closing in on me.

My head is pounding.

My face is sticky from tears.

I think I'm dying…

Panic Attack - Sarah Pingel

I pick up my tea cup;

Sip sip.

The world moves around me as I drink my comfort. The warmth of the sun burns my skin— The wind brushes my hair out of my face— The blue sky reflects off the bird bath in my yard. I sit my tea cup down;

Klink.

My cup clanks against the glass on top my table sending a shiver up my arms. The sun is now dying— The wind is now settling— The once colorful sky is now gray.

Lub Dub.

My heart beats faster, my palms become sweatier.

Thump.

My head pounds, my eyes dart across my backyard full of trees, once green, now dead.

Chatter.

I'm shaking as thoughts cross my mind. What could go wrong if my tea cup broke? What would happen if it began to rain? What if the sun somehow came down and boiled me up? Someone could come over unannounced, killing all the ale this tea and this weather once gave me.

Dub Lub.

Thump.

Chatter.

My heart is in my feet now; It pushes on my toes, sending messages to my brain. I must go inside to hide from this uncertainty; From this unclarity; From this anxiety.

Everyday Life - Sarah Pingel

The earth isn't spinning on its axis anymore.
Oceans are draining into the black void of space.
I can feel the vallied rocks tumbling on top of me;
within me.
Trees are being stolen from their very own roots;
torn up by a black hole.
My brain is morphing into the stars.
My world is ending…

Spacial Breakdown - Sarah Pingel

I never notice the grinding of my teeth until my jaw is aching with soreness.
I never notice I'm pulling the chain on my necklace until there's cuts on my fingers.
I never notice I'm spinning the rings on my fingers until I pinch my swollen skin.
I never care to notice when my anxiety is inflicting pain on myself, because it's the only thing that distracts me from this constant fear of staying alive.

Self Harm - Sarah Pingel

I can feel the sweat on the back of my neck;
slipping down my back.
My underarms are warm,
my thighs are shaking.
Trembles pass through my forehead as it starts to pound.
My eyes must be bloodshot from the lack of blinking I'm
doing.
My lungs are giving out one short breath at a time.
Why did I have to leave the house?
The comfort of isolation.
The warmth of my messy bed piled with blankets and
wrinkled clothes.
Why did I try to exist outside?

Social Anxiety - Sarah Pingel

Distracting myself from my mind is hard.
My head is swirling and tears are dropping.
I can't handle the headache that's starting to form.
Inflicting some hurt onto my physical body
might make my head shut the hell up.
I would do anything to turn my brain off.

The Infliction of Pain - Sarah Pingel

I'm living in a nightmare
called life –
my mindscape is burying me.

My Dreams are Always Nightmares - Sarah Pingel

My eyes are glossed over as I lay in bed.

The hours are passing by.

1:00 am,

2:00 am,

3:00 am.

I can't turn myself off.

Everything I've ever said or ever done is flooding me.

I could have done everything differently.

I wish I would have handled that better.

I should have said something.

Why did I wear that?

I just want to fall asleep…

Anxious Insomniac - Sarah Pingel

My mind cripples me.
I'm scared to be in a relationship —
What if they hate me?
I'm scared to make anyone unhappy —
What if they leave me?
I'm scared to be happy —
What if it's just momentary?
I feel faint at the thought of having to live with my mind
constantly scaring me.

My Mind is a Maze - Sarah Pingel

I feel crazy as my mind tears away at my sanity.

So insane the way I feel when someone looks at me.

When someone breathes near me.

When I have to talk to someone.

When I have to live in this world I was born into.

I'm terrified of your reaction to my existence.

What if You Hate Me - Sarah Pingel

You say,
"Just talk to them,
the worst they could say is *no*."
Exactly.
No could drop out of their mouth and ring in my ear.
My heart will smack the floor like glass falling off a skyscraper.
I will shatter from your small disagreement.
From your slight negative response.
I will scatter as I try to pick myself up again from the thought of you thinking I'm annoying or stupid.
I will glue my cracked self back together even though I know I will continue to push myself off that building time and time again.
Because it's not the *no* that's hurting,
It's the rejection of me in your voice.

Broken Glass - Sarah Pingel

My hands are trembling.
I have to say something.
I need to speak up.
They hurt me.
But if I talk,
they'll be mad at me.
They'll scoff and say something mean.
Heaven only knows the rejection will hurt me worse than
the actual punch did.

Rejection Will Kill Me - Sarah Pingel

I'm so exhausted.

Tears stick to my face as everyone looks at me.

I'm so annoyed at myself for being this way.

I wish I was normal.

Normality is a Lie - Sarah Pingel

I'm sorry I wasn't who you wanted me to be.
I *tried.*
I didn't want to be me either,
but I couldn't help it.
I still can't help it —
This is who I am.
So anxious I can barely function.
So shy I can barely make any friends.
I know you're sick of me,
I'm *sick* of me too.
I'm tired of looking at these tears and hearing this shaking
voice.
I know you don't want me here anymore,
I don't want to be here anymore either.

I'm Sorry for Existing - Sarah Pingel

I don't think I'm scared of dying.

I think I'm scared of the thought of it not being my choice.

Of it not being by my own hand.

Anxiety Feeds my Depression - Sarah Pingel

Depression

I continue my walk as the girl proceeds next to me. Neither of us speaks as our meeting tree becomes a distant memory. We walk through fields of lavender, creeks of multicolored fish, and grassy hills. Her little frame and short legs keep pace with my more mature body as we continue walking. I keep wondering if she is real or if it is just me imagining something familiar so that I can save myself from the misfortune of mental illness.

"Where are we headed?" She asks, tugging at my dress.

"I don't think I'll know until I get there," I answer wholeheartedly. We stop walking when the sun begins to sleep behind the moon. I lay down to look at the stars; she lay down to look at me before shutting her eyes. Grass tickles my bare arms and ankles as I lay on the earth, closing my eyes to try to get some sleep.

As nightly hours pass, thoughts and fears flood my mind. Why was I born? Why doesn't anyone love me enough to see me? Tears begin to fall from my eyes, drenching the ground so much you could swear a flower would blossom there any minute.

"Are you okay?" the girl asks, her eyes narrowing as she opens them, her slumber interrupted by the sounds of weeping.

"I'm okay," I sniffle, the tears not stopping no matter how hard I try to make them. She sits up from the ground and begins lifting me, pulling my arm until I sit up.

"I'm sorry your brain pains you," She says lightly, her grogginess disappearing into thin air as she focuses on me.

"No one even cares how much I want to die," I say breathlessly, soft sobs continuing as I speak. She leans up against me, placing her head on my shoulder as I hold my knees, covering them in tears and snot.

"I'm sorry no one has shown you how important you are. You deserve to live just as much as anyone else. You deserve to bloom, you deserve to rain, you deserve to breathe. You earned a beautiful life just by being alive," She explains slowly, letting the words softly drop out of her mouth.

"I feel as though I don't deserve a life when I don't even appreciate my own heartbeat," I whisper the thought as if it hasn't been plaguing my every belief.

"You don't have to punish yourself for what your brain tells your heart to feel. You do deserve your life, and you deserve to live it free from the harm of depression," My tears begin to lift with her kindness and understanding.

She wraps my hands in hers, and my tears start to dry as
we lie back down to rest for the remainder of the night.

32

Broken.

I feel broken a lot. I feel broken by the people I love. I feel broken by myself. What does it even mean to be broken? Is it when your heart feels like it's in a million pieces? Or is it when you feel so dead inside your heart doesn't make a sound? I don't know which one it is, but I do know I feel both of them.

I feel sad, hurt, alone, stupid.

Gosh,

I feel stupid.

But I mainly feel broken.

Completely and utterly broken.

Broken - Sarah Pingel

You watched me and laughed when I told you I wanted to
leave my body.
You explained to me that I was fine,
great even,
as I was sopping in tears.
You will never understand the agony I felt for years,
as you belittled me and told me my feelings were a sham.
The torture I felt everyday,
waking up to a world I didn't want to be in.
You will never understand how I felt,
because I cannot fully comprehend it either.
I will never be able to grasp the idea that not only did the
people I love fail me,
but also my own brain.

Out of Body - Sarah Pingel

I just wanted to confide in you.

I craved your arms around me while I cried into your warmth.

I just needed you to tell me it was going to be okay,

and even when it wasn't,

you would still be there for me.

But you never said that.

You never held me,

you never comforted me.

I felt so alone.

I felt so abandoned,

even though you were in the same house as me.

You left me to fend for myself even after I begged

for you to tell me I was worth more than death.

But you didn't.

You were silent as I sat in the tub with my head under the water

waiting for my air to run out.

You Helped me Fill the Tub - Sarah Pingel

I beg for your help as water streams down my face.
You hold down my neck,
making me sink beneath my tears.
You lift my head for a brief moment to mock me,
before pushing me back down again
to choke on my own sorrow and salt.

The Torture of Being Unheard - Sarah Pingel

How disgraceful.
To watch your child,
drenched in tears,
begging for your help,
and yet,
you do nothing.
All I wanted was for you
to embrace me.
All I needed was for you
to save me.

Save Me - Sarah Pingel

There's stains on my cheeks from the constant flow of
tears.
Black streaks of mascara run down my face like water-
colors,
quickly flowing off my chin.
If I could just stop crying and wipe my tears,
my face wouldn't look like it has been drawn on
with a permanent marker.

Poisoned Tears - Sarah Pingel

You realize how much
you've cried when your
eyelashes begin to fall out.

Losing Myself - Sarah Pingel

I am a mermaid.

I sleep in the salted waters,

not drowning but learning to live in the environment of

raging H20.

I don't live in the seas though,

I live in my bedroom.

The water doesn't swish around me,

it falls out of my red,

puffy eyes.

H2O - Sarah Pingel

I'm tired,
I'm so tired.
Breathing is so hard,
living is even harder.
It's absolute agony to keep my eyes open.

Breathing is Second Nature - Sarah Pingel

Waking up from a fantastic dream made me realize
that the reality I wake up to every morning
is pointless
compared to the beautiful moment I left behind
when I opened my eyes.

Dreamscape - Sarah Pingel

My room is a mess.
It matches this cramped mind of mine.
I'm trying so hard to stand up,
to change my clothes,
to feel something besides an overwhelming ache in my
chest and in my head.
I feel like I'm being taken over by a parasite that I can
never get better from.
It's as if my room has become my own personal dungeon.

Messy Mind - Sarah Pingel

Monsters don't creep around your room. They creep around your heart. Monsters don't live under your bed. They live silently in your head. Monsters don't feed on your fear. They feed on the happiness you once felt. Monsters don't hunt you in the night. They hunt on your tears and the depression you feel.

Inner Demons - Sarah Pingel

I'm exhausted.

I'm not sure I can keep pushing away the demons in my head.

At some point,

they are going to stop tormenting me so that they can devour me.

They Want to Eat My Heart -Sarah Pingel

It's so hard to tell someone you're depressed. How do you even say it without sounding self-absorbed? I feel like everytime I tell someone how depressed and anxious I am, they just think I'm being dramatic. No matter how loud I cry for help, they always think the same thing. How am I supposed to explain that it physically hurts to live sometimes. My heart is constantly breaking, and my mind is continuously moving. I can't shut off the pain. I can't feel happy most of the time. I can't breathe because my emotions are moving too fast for me to keep control of. I'm hurting so badly, but I can't seem to get anyone to help me. I just want someone to hold me and say it's going to be okay. But I'm laying in my bed alone, crying, and feeling like there's nothing left to hope for.

What Denial Taught Me - Sarah Pingel

I want to spend a day where I'm laughing and the thoughts
of wanting to take my life disappear.
Why can't I have one of those days,
not even one?
There's not a day that goes by that I want to be alive.
Maybe taking everything away will make things better,
maybe leaving this world won't be so bad.
Like falling asleep,
an endless dream,
no reality to wake up to.
I could simply take my life.
No one would notice,
I'm sure,
they'd be happier without my depression to weigh them
down.
They'd be happier without me.

Just One Day - Sarah Pingel

I'm trying so hard to have it all together.
I'm trying to make the tears stop and the pain subside.
I feel like I'm getting burned everytime I try to survive.
Let me die.
Just let me die.

Giving Up - Sarah Pingel

I feel like a ticking time bomb about to detonate myself.
I feel as though I have limited time to live.
There's only so much someone can take before death catches up on them.
I feel like I'm just waiting around and soon enough,
I'm going to explode.

Bomb Squad - Sarah Pingel

I have always been asked what I want my future to look like.

How am I supposed to do that though?

I don't plan on being around for the future.

How am I supposed to try my best for a future I don't want to be a part of?

I just want to be swallowed up by death before the future everyone is talking about becomes my present.

No one seems to care about that though.

No Future - Sarah Pingel

I'm trying.

I'm trying so hard to keep going.

My tears are drowning me.

My heart is crushing me.

No one is protecting me,

And God knows I'm starting to give up fighting to protect

myself.

The Sorrow of Me - Sarah Pingel

So many months,

days,

and minutes

I've spent crying.

I would love to spend just one second smiling.

Calendar Tears - Sarah Pingel

I feel like a caterpillar who never got the chance to form
into a butterfly—
No cocoon to keep me warm.
To keep me safe as I became strong.
My instincts to protect myself have abandoned me.

Metamorphosis - Sarah Pingel

It never ends.

The pain never ceases to exist in me.

My brain is like a storybook without the happily ever after.

My heart is just another organ in my body,

pumping tar instead of blood.

Every morning and every night I lie awake,

while I wait for the grim reaper to join me at the end of

my book.

Once Upon a Time I Died - Sarah Pingel

It must be so comforting

to feel at peace.

Oh how I crave it.

The sweet sound of nothingness.

The warmth of the dirt surrounding me.

The snow in my veins.

How gentle it must feel to have the grim reaper hold my
hand.

How nice it must be to die.

A Forever Dream - Sarah Pingel

I think about going to a field.
A pretty one, with flowers blooming all around me.
I think about wearing a white dress.
One that flows down my legs until it reaches my ankles.
I think about sitting there for hours.
Soaking up every last bit of the sun.
I think about taking my last breath in that field,
in that dress,
with the sunlight beating down on my porcelain skin.
I think about dying.

My Last Adventure - Sarah Pingel

Self Loathing

Waking under the sun, birds chirping in the fair sky, the breeze rustling with the loose leaves on the ground, and the sound of water flowing echoing from a distance. The girl and I look at one another with gentle smiles before continuing our journey. We're walking longer than we had the day before, not stopping even once to catch our breath.

"Should we find something to eat and drink?" She asks. Hesitantly, I agree with a nod and follow her into the forest of bushels ahead of us. We continue our steady pace until the girl stops in front of a bush of berries surrounding a pond full of crystal-clear water.

"Is this alright?" She proposed as she pointed toward a bunch of blackberries. I nod as I look at the bubbles fish are leaving behind beneath the glass surface they were swimming in.

"Okay," I reluctantly say, finally looking at the fruit she offered me. She's now sitting down next to the shrubs, picking around the thorns to reach the pinnacle of fruit.

"Wouldn't you like any?" She mutters as she munches away, her mouth turning purple with each bite. I look at myself through the reflection of the water and begin to feel nauseated with disgust for what was looking back at me.

I suppose I didn't always hate myself or my body, but at some point, I started to loathe it. The freckles that sat on my face made me feel dirty, and the way my nose arched made me feel ugly. I especially hated my stomach and the way it rolled when I wasn't sucking it in. I looked at myself every morning when I woke and every night before bed, stripping my clothes off to get a complete picture of myself in the mirror. *Disgusting*, I would tell myself as tears rolled down my face. I hate my body, I hate my face, and I hate who I am.

Pulling myself out of thought to look away from the water again, the girl stared at me intently, her hands still full of blackberries, but she wasn't eating them anymore. I stare at her momentarily before realizing she had asked me if I wanted any a while ago, and I hadn't answered her yet.

"No, it's okay; you can have them," I answer nervously, my stomach indicating that I am just as hungry as she is.

"There's plenty for us both," she insisted, showing me the ripe pile she held. I looked at her and back at these beautifully grown berries. I imagined they'd taste like how Summer feels. I know, though, that for me, they would taste like regret and feel like all the hurt in the world was entering my body.

"I'm okay, I'm not hungry," I state untruthfully.

"Your belly says differently," She pesters.

"I don't want any. Thank you, though," I insist, once again, stubbornly. She stands up and brushes the purple pieces off her once white, now stained, dress. She looks at me, still having to tilt her head even though she is now standing. Deep in thought, she stares into my eyes until finally breaking our eye contact to look at the cloudless sky.

"Do you think the earth hates itself?" She asks bluntly.

"No," I answer, looking up at the radiant blueness with her.

"But what about the ugly things on earth? Such as the cracks in the ground or the moss-colored mud in swamps?" She questions.

"Those are all just things that make each part of the earth uniquely its own and uniquely beautiful," I explain, questioning her motives for asking me these questions. We stood there momentarily, watching the birds fly above us as they tweeted at each other.

"Then why do you believe you are ugly?" She defends as she stops looking up and begins to look at me again. Her eyes fixated on my expression as I began to cry deeply, the tears flooding out of me as quickly as that sentence dropped out of her mouth.

"I don't know how to see myself any differently," I wept, emerging from my cracked heart. I've hated myself for so long; I don't know what it feels like to feel loved in the presence of my own eyes."

It's like a flowing motion, hating yourself. How you look, speak, move. Like muscle memory telling me to stay home, away from the world. It is a never-ending cycle of hatred for the person I see in the mirror every day when I wake up and every night when I go to sleep. I judge everything about myself, from the red splotches that show even more so because of my light skin to the tangles in my thin hair that stay no matter how much I brush it. I'm just a girl with a head full of doubt and sorrow eating me away as if a child who loved themself never existed here.

"You are a snowflake in a world full of snow," she says. Each snowflake forms, falls, and melts in its own way, at its own pace. You are perfectly you in every way, and there's no one else who gets to be that," she assures me, soothing my heart with her soft words.

"What if I can never see myself that way?" I sigh, my tears beginning to slow down and dry up.

"You will with each new breath you breathe and each new step you take. Loving yourself will become easier every day, and soon enough, your snowflake will form in your eyes too," She vows, confidence and acceptance beaming off of her like the sun does when it reflects off a frozen lake. I look at my reflection again and smile as we sit together next to the bush full of fruit and the small body of shining water. She wipes my last tear with her purple-stained hand as I finally eat the blackberry her other hand gives me.

I wish I was happier with myself,
but I fear I will always hate the person I see.

62

Looking at Myself - Sarah Pingel

I watch as other girls with the same name as me
live greater lives than I do.
They talk about their interest with smiles beaming off of
them
while their multitudes of friends listen with love.
They walk with confidence in their vintage clothes
while people search in every thrift store for the same
outfit.
Their skin is gleaming; their hair is shining.
The sun hits them so perfectly.
I wish I was one of those Sarah's,
but I'm plain Jane.
My freckles don't sit like theirs; my eyes aren't as
beautiful of a blue either.
My hair is frizzy; my clothes are lumpy.
I think my parents made a mistake naming me.
I can't live up to the beauty of all the other girls I meet
with my name.
Oh to be as lovely as them.

Sarah Jane - Sarah Pingel

It feels as if my heart was burning.
Looking at this body of mine,
how it rolls,
how it arches.
I wish I felt pretty.
I wish this body of mine made me smile.
Instead,
it makes me want to disappear.

My Figure is Burning - Sarah Pingel

I don't think I love you anymore.

You're not the little girl you once were.

You don't beam in the light—

things don't make you happy anymore.

Not like they used to at least…

I think I hate you now.

Your image and your thoughts.

At this point,

I can't remember even loving you in the first place.

The Little Girl Within is Gone - Sarah Pingel

Through my eyes,

I see someone I don't like.

I see a stranger.

I didn't gain this weight.

I don't remember having this crooked nose.

Who stole the body I had?

Who ripped at the face I thought I liked?

Who is the girl in this shattered mirror of mine?

Body Dysmorphia - Sarah Pingel

"I hate you!" I shout.
"I hate you,"
"I hate you…"
"I hate you."
Tears smother my face
as my reflection stares back at me.

Hatred - Sarah Pingel

I pour the liquor down my throat,

trying to forget you.

You're meaningless,

yet your words hurt me more than anyone else's.

I *hate* you.

I pour the liquor down my throat,

so that I can't see you.

So that the mirror becomes blurry,

and you can't stare back at me anymore.

I pour the liquor down my throat,

to drown out the drunken images of myself.

Drunk Thoughts - Sarah Pingel

The earth doesn't have a single substance to help me,
to stop me from hating myself.
I want to die every moment I wake up,
and every moment I go to sleep.

Vodka Can't Stop the Loathing Dreams - Sarah Pingel

I could just cry,

hearing myself speak.

My voice is so melodramatic as words drain out of my mouth.

No wonder no one wants to help me.

No wonder no one cares to shake me out of this dreadful mindset of mine.

I can hear myself muffle sobs and screeching words.

I wouldn't want to help me either...

Ugly Uttering - Sarah Pingel

I feel this overwhelming feeling of blankness.
Every feeling is still there,
but they're muffled,
as if they were distant whispers just trying to make themselves heard.

I Feel Like Stock Paper - Sarah Pingel

The tears make my face numb.

Numb of everything but the sticky feeling it leaves behind on my swollen-red cheeks.

After crying I feel as if I'm drifting through the world emotionless.

My limp body carrying me until the next time pain sneaks its way in,

bringing back all the betraying feelings my form once felt.

Floating Above My Dead Body - Sarah Pingel

I gag at the taste of food,

yet I continue to shove it down my throat.

Sobbing on the kitchen floor,

I eat.

I want to feel something,

anything,

even if that feeling is just being able to taste a peach or swallow a spoonful of cereal.

Not being able to feel anything is the bane of my existence.

So I cry as I force myself to chew,

so that maybe,

I can feel.

Binge Eating - Sarah Pingel

I turn off the lights so I can't see myself,

my body,

my thoughts.

I'm such a betrayal to myself.

I hate the person I see because the woman basking in the

sunlight,

Isn't loved,

Isn't wanted,

Isn't happy.

I close the curtains and hide under the covers,

so that I can't see the control my screwed up brain has on

me.

I Only See Disgust in the Mirror - Sarah Pingel

I'm so envious of every other woman.
How they look,
talk,
act.
I'm so sick of looking at myself,
hearing myself,
watching myself.
I'm so jealous of every girl that isn't me.

Jealousy - Sarah Pingel

My Mawmaw and I have the same size ring fingers–
I think because we were molded from the same clay
with the same idea in mind.
The red that dances in her brown hair
also dances in mine.
Her blue eyes shimmer like the deep sea,
as do mine.
Her skills and her passions flow through me
like a damned creek about to burst.
I love her so much…
I wonder why it's so hard for me to love myself,
when I am her.
She is the magic I lack.

She is More Than I Could Ever Be - Sarah Pingel

My brain takes over my body like moss takes over a forest.

Its weeds grow through me,

making thorns stab my heart.

I can't bear the pain my head causes my body.

Thoughts linger in my ear,

telling me I'm worth nothing,

telling me my body is deformed and my mind is crazy.

Tears roll down my face,

passing each freckle as they jump off my chin.

It's hard to love myself,

when toxins are flowing through my brain.

Theres Toxic Waste in Me - Sarah Pingel

How do I explain to you that your words have wounded
me?
I try to tell you,
but it's as if my voice is on mute.
You say to *grow up* and stop thinking badly of myself,
yet just yesterday you told me I looked *fat*.
You tell me to eat less,
to run more.
You pretend you're not hurting me by saying you are just
trying to help.
I have begged for you to save me for years but to no avail,
you never came.
At this point,
I already hate myself enough without your help.

Your Judgment - Sarah Pingel

At some point,

I stopped pretending I wasn't hungry.

At some point,

the hunger became so regular,

I couldn't feel it anymore.

I Think I have Anorexia - Sarah Pingel

I feel guilty when I eat.

Every bite makes me want to die,

every swallow makes me sick to my stomach.

I can hear the calories as I chew,

it's as if I was scratching my fingernails across a chalkboard.

It hurts so badly to make my stomach full.

Anorexia is Eating my Hunger - Sarah Pingel

It's so unappealing,
food.
I can't stand chewing it.
I can't stand swallowing it.
My brain is sending my stomach signals,
but I choose to ignore them.
I want to be skinny—
who cares if I die trying?

Signal Error - Sarah Pingel

The moon shines down on my freckled face.
Clouds cover every inch of the midnight sky,
leaving nothing but my figure shadowed across the ground.
Trees moan as the wind pushes against them.
I watch as leaves flow through the wind,
I wish I was a leaf.
Dying in the fall and being reborn in the spring.
Maybe then I could shed the world of myself,
and bring forth actual beauty.

Autumn - Sarah Pingel

I lie here

imagining what it would be like to live within the stars,

to sit on the moon as my body blends into the sky.

I dream to be up there

away from the suffering and this aching feeling I have in

my soul.

I want to be a shooting star so that I can escape myself.

I Want to Become the Galaxy - Sarah Pingel

Do it.

Place the bullets in the gun.

Tell me to think peaceful thoughts.

Close my eyes as I drift away.

Don't try to save me,

please don't.

Let me leave,

let me escape,

I don't want to be dead on the inside if it doesn't match

the decaying on the outside.

I don't want to talk,

I don't want to move,

I don't want to breathe.

Let me go.

Let me sink beneath the beating of my own heart.

I'm Suffering - Sarah Pingel

Even though her body
was extremely cruel to her,
she was still afraid to go.

Help My Trembling Hands - Sarah Pingel

I'm so sick of being alone.

I'm so tired of hearing my voice echo.

No one wants to be around me,

not even me.

I would dig my grave,

but no one would come to my funeral anyway.

My Funeral will be Haunted by my Ghost - Sarah Pingel

My body betrays me.

It screams in my ear that I'm worthless.

It manipulates my brain to think I shouldn't be in this
world.

It looks in the mirror and tells me I'm disproportionate.

I sob into my pillow,

leaving mascara and salty tears all over my face.

Shut up,

I yell at myself.

I wish just once,

my body wouldn't betray me.

I Can't Find Myself Within These Betrayals - Sarah Pingel

Betrayal

We slept for hours after eating those bushels of berries, not waking until the sun yelled at our eyes. Forcing ourselves up before continuing on our feet. We continue through grass so thick it prickles through our dresses and so tall it tickles our knees. We go past creeks flowing so high that I give the girl a piggyback ride, leaving her dress bone dry and mine soaked, sticking to my legs. Finally, we reach the edge of nature. Busy roads and loud people begin to drown out the sound of freedom, the sound of peace. I pause at the road leading to the noise, the girl joining me in my halt, standing still beside me. I sit on the last bit of land that isn't tainted by humans, the girl joining me again, mirroring my movements.

"I don't want to go out there," I confess.

"Don't you want to be around more people?" She asks.

"Not really…" I mutter faintly.

"Why not?"

"People are cruel," I growl, pausing for a second before speaking again, "I'm cruel…" She sat for a second, looking at the people walking around, laughing, talking, living life.

"Humans love so deeply yet always seem to hurt themselves and others around them… You can't control how someone treats you, but you can choose how to live your best life despite their behavior. You can choose to become the light, even if you're being pushed into the dark. You can choose forgiveness amid anger," She advises, her eyes still wondering the town we sat upon.

"I hoped to stay kind throughout all the pain, but I didn't," I reply softly.

Betrayal is a funny thing. You never realize you're doing it to the people closest to you until it's too late, and you never feel the knife flying at your own back until it cuts you. I had been stabbed so many times growing up I became numb to it for a while. I let everyone I loved eat my soul whole. I let strangers step on my legs until I couldn't move. I let boys spit on my heart. With all the hatred I already had for myself, I began not thinking about others' feelings or how the things I did affect them. I lost my way in a pool of people drowning me, me drowning them, and me drowning myself.

"You are still growing," She smiles, "You're not meant to respond perfectly the first time someone hurts you. You aren't born planning to hurt someone else, either. You question yourself and not just others, which shows how kind you already are, even with your mistakes." I listen to her voice, so childlike yet still so grown up, nasally and calm-sounding, too, like mine.

"I'm afraid of others… I'm afraid of myself," I tell her with a crack in my shaky voice. I pause for a moment as she watches me, somehow knowing I have to process my following words.

"I'm so anxious about the world and the people in it. I'm so anxious about myself. What if I can't handle this pounding in my chest?" The words finally fall out as my hands begin to tremble.

"If you're choosing every day to be better, you don't have to be afraid of anyone else or yourself. You don't have to be fearless; you just have to want to be better with every day that comes and hope others choose that path too," She pauses for barely even a second to breathe in, "Anxiety is a part of you, and it hurts, but you can do it. You can fight it and stand tall; I know you can. No matter how much it pinches you, pinch it back and tell your brain that you won't let it define you or your life," She smiles as she tells me with so much affirmation and clarity, you would think she did research about *The Betrayals of the Human Mind*.

I brush my brunette hair behind my ears as the wind pulls at it, tranquility spilling over me like a wave covering the once-dry sand on a beach. The girl grinned at me as if she was feeling exactly what I was feeling. I chuckle at her vast grin, seeds from our previous feast stuck in her teeth. She picks at the leftover food in her mouth and then begins cackling back at me as she points at the seeds stuck in my teeth, too. We were beaming, looking at each other, tears of laughter falling from our eyes. Finally resting our heads against each other, she nestled in the crevice of my neck as I lay my head on top of hers; we stayed like that, watching the same energetic city we had recently come upon continue with their lives.

I've learned that no one really wants me,
they just want my soul and they'll drink from
my heart until I'm empty.

Empty Vessel - Sarah Pingel

I heard the breathless whispers when I walked past a crowd.

I saw the glares as people spread lies about me.

I read the messages calling me a whore,

calling me easy,

calling me ugly to dig in the hurt a little more.

All because I liked the wrong boy.

The Heartache of a False Rumor- Sarah Pingel

I stayed home and cried myself to sleep every night for
weeks after you broke my heart—
Not just because of the lies you told and the rumors you
started,
but because I honestly liked you.
How you laughed with me and held me tight,
I never realized you only did those things behind a screen
or a closed door.
You were cute with your stupid clothes and your charming
smile,
so I never put the puzzle pieces together that you were just
using me as a joke.
I wish I didn't have to be humiliated for you and your
friends to have a good time though.
I wish you would have just left me alone.

I Was Just a Prank - Sarah Pingel

What regret I have for letting you into my life.
For letting you near my home,
near my heart.
I can't believe I trusted your blue eyes.
I was so stupid to let you kiss my lips,
to let you caress my hand with your thumb.
I feel terrible for letting myself like you.

I Regret Knowing You - Sarah Pingel

My heart sits on my sleeve.
People poke fun at me,
at my emotions.
They say I'm being over dramatic,
the rumors wouldn't hurt anyone else this badly,
they say—
As if that makes the pain go away,
as if I can control my heart strings ripping apart.
I feel like I can't breathe as I hear my name
drop out of others' mouths.
Who cares though?
I'm just sensitive.

Crying is for Babies - Sarah Pingel

It hurts to cry. It feels like fire. Opening up old wounds. It makes my throat sore and my head pound. Yet I can't stop. I can't stop crying. Tears just leak from me like a broken fossett. My heart is so heavy. It lowers down like an anchor to the ship of my life. I'm completely hurt in every possible way. It's so hard to last in a place that wants you to go away even more than your heart wants you to. So many cracks are in my small physique. Too many for my body to handle.

I'm Decaying - Sarah Pingel

His words spread like wildfire.

The fake and tasteless rumors erupted out of him like an active volcano.

You were like a sister to me,

yet you continued to speak to him as if nothing was wrong.

As if you didn't watch me cry myself to sleep,

as if you didn't watch as I hid myself from society for weeks.

It hurt so badly that at the same time you were consoling me,

you were entertaining a friendship with him.

I didn't know at the time,

but now looking back I can see,

that the moment the gossip came out,

was the beginning of me losing my friend.

I Didn't Expect to Lose You - Sarah Pingel

Take a bite of me,

take a bite of my world.

Swallow my pain,

swallow my poison.

Might as well eat me whole,

for you have never cared if I dissolve anyways.

I'm Poisonous - Sarah Pingel

You're like the snow,
everytime warmth tries to seize you,
you melt away.
You're beautiful,
but cold.

Snowglobe - Sarah Pingel

I think your treachery hurts the most
because I trusted you more than anything or anyone else
on this planet.
Like a deer trusts a meadow,
I had confidence in your love for me.
Until I saw the light of the gun,
pointed at my head.

Wounded by You - Sarah Pingel

I can't handle how you see me.

You roll your eyes and giggle as I walk by.

You message me saying how stupid I look.

You make me cry myself to sleep.

I can't handle how you make my stomach turn.

I wish you would stop crushing me.

I'm just a girl.

I'm just *one* fucking girl.

One in a Crowd of Thousands - Sarah Pingel

I don't understand how I got to this point in my life.

To the point where people hate me for mere rumors.

To the point where I cry myself to sleep not just because

I loathe myself

but because others do too,

because you do.

You spit at me with your words,

yet just the other night you were begging me for some

action.

Is it because I didn't want to?

I feel like a fool falling for you.

I feel like I died and this is *hell*.

I'm Burning at the Accusations of Being a Witch -

Sarah Pingel

I'm kind,

I think…

I'm well liked,

when I can benefit someone else.

I put everyone's happiness above my own,

which can sometimes make my own wants blurred and

pushed to the side.

I am called sweet,

so caring.

I am called a doormat,

so easy to walk over.

The world will never accept my heart unless it is to benefit

their own will.

I will continue to put people first,

until the day that it kills me.

I'm a People Pleaser - Sarah Pingel

Epsom salt surrounds my pained body as I cry.
The salt in my tears mixes with the salt in the tub
as water covers my sinking face.
People make my head throb and my throat ache,
I just want to close my eyes and go away.

I Smell Lavender Salt as I Drown - Sarah Pingel

Do not speak to me as if you know me.

You do not have the right to speak on my behalf.

You do not have the right to look at me with disapproving eyes.

Shut your mouth and close your eyes,

you have no right to even know my name.

You Don't Know Me - Sarah Pingel

You're not my friend.

You're not my acquaintance.

You're nothing to me now.

Why do you insist on belittling me?

You laugh with me one day and then talk behind my back
another.

You call me your companion to my face and then betray
me by running to amoral people who have once used a
knife to carve out my heart.

How do you call yourself a good person,

and then treat the people who love you the way you do?

You're never going to be a good man,

if you never make the choice to do better.

You Insult my Kindness Everyday - Sarah Pingel

My body feels sick from you touching it.
I remember your fingertips gliding under the elastic of my
underwear and I want to cry.
Tears began to build up the farther down you went,
I couldn't handle it anymore,
so I pushed you away.
You said you understood as I asked you to leave,
and then you told the world I begged you to fuck me,
that I went all the way with you.
My knees hit the ground as I heard the whispers about my
virginity.
I didn't let you take it,
I barely let you see it.
But now I have to live the rest of my life with a sense of
shame.
Because even though I never let you inside of me,
people will always think I did.
And that makes me feel violated—
it always will.

I was Never Yours - Sarah Pingel

I remember like it was yesterday.

A cold night,

so cold in fact,

the tip of my nose showed red.

The wind pinched me as I pushed your lips away,

you kept trying anyway.

"Please stop,"

I ask of you,

but you insist your lips need to touch mine.

I resistantly agree and let you graze me,

tears filling my eyes.

It will be over soon,

I tell myself.

But that second long kiss,

felt like a lifetime,

in darkness.

No Feelings for Your Insistence - Sarah Pingel

Unfamiliar hands,
rough and aged,
grasp my waist.
My eyes widened
as I turned to face an elderly man.
He asks what my tattoo says
as his fingers run across the ink.
I backed from his grip
as he watched me run off.
I turn around with fear,
he is grinning,
thinking he did nothing wrong.

Disrespectful Hands - Sarah Pingel

How do you look at me,
a young girl,
and crave what you see?
How do you sexualize me
and comment on my appearance
as I sit there uncomfortably?
You say such vulgar things,
it seems a sin that you're allowed to be near me.
I feel violated by your eyes,
I feel dirty when you speak.
I'm afraid of you
and your intentions with me.

I'm the Same Age as Your Daughter - Sarah Pingel

I stare at my breast in the mirror. They topple over as I unclip my bra, sagging and showing all the stretch marks they've endured ever since they grew on my chest in fifth grade. Their warmth seeps into my hands as I hold them, they're all mine.

I stare at my breast in the mirror. Why is it that when a man goes topless it's seen as normal, but if I were to take off my blouse, I would be seen as a slut and a whore.

"Cover your nipples!!" They scream at me, as they ignore the naked man walking by.

I stare at my breast in the mirror. My cleavage shows in most of my clothing, so I must be easy. I have big boobs, so I must be asking for it when a man touches me without my permission. It's obvious that I have breasts, so it must be okay when men comment promiscuous things about them.

I stare at my breast in the mirror and I cry. I cry because when I'm naked, looking in the mirror all I see is the only thing men have ever wanted from me. They want what they can't have, and then once they feel the touch of my soft breast, they leave. They don't care about me.

My thoughts.

My dreams.

They only care about my boobs rubbing against them as we kiss. Men have never loved me for my heart, they've always just loved what sits on top of it.

I stare at my breast in the mirror. They're supposed to be mine, loved by me, cherished by my body, yet I hate them. I seem to invite betrayals into my life just by being *"gifted"* with these things hanging off of me. To many of the men I've met, these balls of fat on my chest are an invite for them to have their way with me.

My Breast - Sarah Pingel

It hurts so bad.

My chest feels like it's cracking.

Like my skin is peeling off to reveal a dead heart.

I don't understand what I did to deserve such betrayals,

from strangers,

from friends,

from family.

It would be more humane to just kill me now

instead of making me feel this agony.

I'm Aching - Sarah Pingel

I never had a particularly *terrible* childhood.

I had homemade meals made for me from the hardworking hands of my mother,

her back aching—unknowingly so through the eyes of her children;

sometimes her pain getting the best of her until she broke.

My dad kept the roof above my head and the clothes on my back,

his mind unintentionally cracking as he worked through the storms he internally faced;

sometimes his upbringing getting the best of him until his anger balled its fist.

My sisters and I were as close as sisters could be growing up,

we tried to stick together as we all shared different versions of the same childhood;

sometimes our cracked hearts and fragile minds getting the best of us until we ripped at each other's insecurities.

That home kept me alive,

yet it still bared its teeth at me until I was shredded into nothing more than a torn up entity.

Until I was nothing more than an irrelevant,

expendable.

Underlying Abuse - Sarah Pingel

I feel like such a burden—
to myself,
to the ones who supposedly love me,
to people I don't even know.
By just existing,
I am too much for everyone around me—
a weight for them to carry.
I want to be worth something.
I want to believe I'm meant to be here.
I don't know why I'm alive if I'm just going to spend my
life
miserable to others and to myself.

I Was a Mistake - Sarah Pingel

I'm a reckless driver.
I let people pull me in every direction.
I let myself wreck into a mountain.
Because maybe if I get damaged enough,
the hurt won't be as painful.

Accidents Happen Everyday - Sarah Pingel

I'm shy,

I don't stand up for myself.

I need to be more confident.

When I'm outgoing,

I'm too talkative and annoying.

I need to shut up sometimes.

I'm so tired of not knowing who I'm supposed to be for each person in this god forsaken world.

I never seem to pick the side of me that people want around.

How am I supposed to live my life if everyone treats me like I'm always wrong?

I'm so tired of being me because being me is never right.

I'm an Introverted Extrovert - Sarah Pingel

She tries so hard to please the ones around her.

She breaks herself in every way to make others smile.

She puts herself last every single time.

Yet when she's hurting,

the world still turns its back on her.

Love isn't Returned When I'm the One Crying

– Sarah Pingel

I knew you.

You were the girl in the cardigans everyday.

You were the person I always wanted to be around.

You were all mine.

I ruined it,

I let you down,

At the time

I didn't realize what I was doing.

But I know I betrayed you,

and that kills me.

My Wilted Flower - Sarah Pingel

There's a weight in my chest. It pushes on my heart and makes tears descend from my eyes. Salty tears that burn after crying so much. I feel so let down. I feel so useless. Why am I such an insect to other people? Why am I always beaten down? I don't understand how people can make a person feel this way. So broken and alone. I hate this feeling. The beating of my heart doesn't speak anymore. It just mellows to the sound of the water leaving my eyes.

I'm Lonely - Sarah Pingel

I hope I die soon.

I hope I get to go to sleep and never wake up.

I want away from the betrayals of people that are supposed to love me,

that are supposed to have my back and support me.

I'm so sick of being nice to everyone,

putting everyone above myself and trusting that they'll take care of my heart like I always have theirs.

I'm so tired of being beaten down by not just people who hate me,

but by people who are supposed to love me.

I Need Mercy - Sarah Pingel

If I am hated for simply living,

let the heavens above bring me home.

If I am excluded for simply being,

lay my soul to rest in the ground beneath my feet.

If I am such a burden,

let the mounds of dirt smother me until I am no more.

Let Me Go - Sarah Pingel

I feel so smothered by the unreciprocated love of those around me.

By unfeeling friends and cruel romances,

by clueless family members and purposeful strangers.

I give so much of myself wrapped in a bow for others to rip apart at with a grin,

I crave love and acceptance.

I pine after the dream to be wanted by someone.

Please Hold Me - Sarah Pingel

My heart was made too big for this world.

It sits on my sleeve as people rip at it.

They stomp it to the ground,

and then ask me why I don't take better care of it.

My heart holds together with bandages

as I sit it back in my chest.

I weep as I wait for the next person to steal it from me.

I wait for someone else to call me a pushover.

I wait for them to say I'm too nice,

that I deserve for my heart to be thrown around.

I must deserve to be crushed.

Eventually I'm Going to Shatter - Sarah Pingel

Why does everyone think I can survive on my own?

I'm not strong,

I'm just one girl in a world full of hatred.

I'm so exhausted from the tears and the constant trying.

All I do is let myself crumble to hold up everyone else.

I'm just one person,

why isn't anyone stopping me?

Why isn't anyone helping me?

I'm losing control of the will to keep going.

My Controls Aren't Working - Sarah Pingel

To breathe in this world,

is to also have pain.

To be trusting,

is to be betrayed.

To be loving,

is to be hurt.

To be attentive,

is to be forgotten.

To be caring,

is to be hated.

The people who once said they would always be there,

stab you in the back with the same knife,

they were supposed to protect you with.

Life isn't Pretty - Sarah Pingel

I'm afraid.

I can't lie and say I'm not.

I feel like I'm all alone.

I just wish I wasn't here anymore.

I don't want to be here anymore.

I have no one.

No one that actually loves me.

I'm never enough,

I'm never important or necessary for anyone.

I just want to be held and told that I matter.

I don't understand why I'm never good enough.

I'm so tired of living in this kind of place.

No one sees how lost I am.

I just get blamed,

yelled at,

lectured,

or left.

I don't know what to do.

Everything's a blur.

I feel so worthless.

I don't know how much longer I can hold on.

I'm so Lonesome - Sarah Pingel

My heart is sad.

It weeps like a willow tree on a gusty fall night.

Its tears rush down like niagara falls,

pounding into the ground.

My heart is sad for the life I lived.

It hurts endlessly

from the people that entered my life at such a young

and delicate age.

My heart wallows in my pain.

In the betrayals I've faced before even becoming an adult,

in the screams I endured while sitting on the bathroom

floor.

In all the anxiety,

depression,

and loneliness I've faced.

My heart breaks for the innocence of a sixteen year old

me

No Childhood - Sarah Pingel

Healing

The girl began to walk in the direction we were originally going, towards the busybodies and paved roads, before looking back to see if I was following her. I stand still, not moving toward her, not moving away from her.

"Did you want to go a different way?" She wonders.

"I think I know where I was headed when we met," I admit as she walks back toward me, looking at my face as my brows soften.

"I was planning on…" I pause, worried she will be disappointed in me for thinking such things. She watches me as I stand there staring back at her, my eyes sturdy and my mind running wild.

"At some point, I just stopped planning for my future. I stopped hoping for happiness or looking for someone to love me. When it all came down to it, the child I was supposed to be and the teen body I was supposed to flourish in died without even being buried." I explain, "So I guess I decided I would finally end it all." She listens closely to every word I speak, her deep blue eyes flickering in the sunlight as she begins to walk towards me; grabbing my hand with a tight squeeze,

"It's okay. I know…" She replies, pulling me to follow her.

We begin walking back towards the way we came, neither of us making a peep the rest of the time as our hands stay clasped together. We stride past the bushes full of blackberries and the stems we left over. We stroll past the meadow of lavender, the flowing stream of fish, and the mountains of grass. Soon enough, we stood upon the tree that started our journey. It felt like it took us days to leave its view, yet mere moments to get back under its watchful eye. Turning to face me the same way we met and letting me out of her grasp, the girl stood just five feet away from me once again.

"How did you know?" I ask, finally breaking our silence.

"I came with you because I wanted to remind you why you shouldn't leave a life that you deserve to flourish in," She responds. My heart felt as though it had stopped, and yet it was pounding so hard in my chest that I swore it could bust out at any moment.

"I feel guilty for breathing. I feel guilty because sometimes I still don't want to be breathing." I cry out, "Why do I deserve to be here still? Why am I gifted life when all I've ever wished for was to be *dead?* All I ever craved was the strength to end myself because I didn't think I had the strength to keep living. I feel so ashamed of myself for still being here on this earth even though I know I want to keep fighting," I whimper as my heart sinks to my feet and crocodile tears fall out of my eyes. The girl stares at me in loving sorrow.

"You deserve every happiness, and you deserve to be here. You have to remember that, even when your head says you don't," She soothes, reaching up to wipe my tears again with her soft, petite hands. Getting on my knees to be at her height, I hug the girl tightly as she hugs me back.

"Thank you… for everything," I whisper.

"I'll always be with you, Jane, forever." She says as she backs away from me with another gentle smile. "Wait!" I exclaim, grabbing her hand one more time. "Please wait, I don't want to forget you." Our eyes dampen with tears as the sun brightens behind her frame.

"Aster," She states tenderly, "I'm Aster." Her name strikes me to the core. *Aster;* my star, my flower. So full of wisdom, love, and faith. She's all *mine,* she's *me*. The sun begins to turn Aster into the petals, her hand squeezing mine one last time before entirely disappearing into the sky.

One last tear falls from my eye as I feel her in the wind that rushes around me. My heart starts beating rhythmically in my chest for the first time in forever; my

eyes ignite with an amount of hope I've never felt before.
I can finally feel the light shining within me.

I *choose* to live.

Fifteen flowers loop around my head as I try to grasp the feeling of healing.

Their colorful petals swing around my body, telling me to forgive myself and the people who have harmed me.

Fifteen flowers die in the fall, as they wait for me to grow. The same fifteen flowers bloom back in the spring, excitingly welcoming the new me.

The Fifteenth Flower - Sarah Pingel

The strength of healing is breathing in the fresh air of the
world
and knowing everything is going to be okay,
even when it feels like your life is falling apart.

The Wind Will Brush Past You - Sarah Pingel

I'm terrified to heal,
not because I don't want to,
but because I don't know who I am without constant pain.
I don't remember a happy version of myself.
My whole life has been me sinking beneath the surface of
a world I didn't want to be in.
I don't know who I am without an anchor on my heart.
It's scary for me to get better because what if it doesn't
last?
What if I go back to the torture I've always endured?
What if happiness is just a dream of mine,
and the only comfort I'll ever be able to feel is in the arms
of the normality of my depression?
It's terrifying trying to feel better,
because I never know if I'll end up worse.
But I'm going to keep fighting for myself.
For the life I want.

The Fight Within - Sarah Pingel

After tragedy,

that sigh of relief when you've finished crying

is most possibly,

the most relieving thing I've ever felt.

The Relief in the Aftermath - Sarah Pingel

Your hands glide against the keys of a piano.
Your voice echoes throughout this creaking house.
You sit me down next to you and say,
write.
You say,
sing.
Suddenly,
my tears dry.
My heart mends.
It might just be for the mere moments
we are writing music together,
but I feel safe.
I feel at home.

My Sister is Apollo - Sarah Pingel

It's okay that you didn't see my broken heart.

It's alright that you didn't know how to help me back then.

You were just a child yourself.

I don't blame you for being afraid,

I don't hate you for pushing me away.

You have become my closest companion in recent years,

you have made up for everything,

by just helping me now.

Sisterhood - Sarah Pingel

The healing I was able to do was because of you.
You experienced pain with me as we grew into adults.
We shared tears and traumas,
you carried me as I carried you.
I watched you fight the way your brain makes you hurt,
and find your way to happiness.
I'm thankful to have you through life.
Thank you.

Roo - Sarah Pingel

With how much I've grown,
I've come to realize something.
All those times I begged for you,
truly would have saved me years of agony,
if you would have just opened your eyes.
Now that I have you to hold me,
and to now know how peaceful that feels,
I know I could have started healing way sooner in life.
I forgive you,
I love you,
but it's okay that I'm never going to forget that.

Hug Me Until the Past Disappears- Sarah Pingel

Blackberry bushes poke me as I snatch at their sweetness.
You wipe my tears and nibble my forehead while you
pluck the thorns from my doll-like hands.
When my midnight hunger hits,
you fill bowls with milk and cereal for the both of us.
While we feast,
you teach me how to read;
with a story about a tree.
You covered my cuts in bandages and watched as they
healed.
You tried to sew my gashes with needle and thread,
but it just left scars.
The pain still flows through me,
but it's easier because of you.
My water lily.

Mammy - Sarah Pingel

I haven't cried in days,

in weeks,

in months.

I've broken down,

I've gotten back up,

and now I'm okay.

Maybe not perfect,

but I'm okay.

Trying Through Time - Sarah Pingel

The good moments are what help my soul to heal—
Remembering that even though I never felt great,
there were still good times.
I'm thankful for those moments that bad thoughts weren't
taking up my mind,
because those moments were so pure,
and they're the reason I'm able to move on now.

Grateful Moments - Sarah Pingel

Wind blows through my hair
traveling down my spine
and wrapping around my ankles.
It feels nice to feel the wind touch my skin.
It feels nice to be alive.
To *want* to be alive.

I Want to Feel the Wind - Sarah Pingel

Gosh I missed it.
The flowers in the Spring,
the sun in the Summer.
The birds chirping,
the bees buzzing.
The green grass growing around every tree,
the water dancing overtop every little pebble.
Gosh,
I missed it,
happiness.
What it felt like,
looked like,
sounded like.
I missed it so much.

Happy - Sarah Pingel

On the days I tell myself it's time for me to go, he licks my tears and lays beside me. On the nights I cry myself to sleep, his head rests by mine and his paw touches my hand. On the days I'm angry at the world, he sits in the rearview mirror and makes me remember my laugh. At the moments it's almost too much to bear, I look at him and I smile. My pained soul will always be a part of me, and I'm thankful I have him to help me heal each time it comes to pass.

My soul dog - Sarah Pingel

I look at you as tears spill over me.
Your soft golden eyes watch me closely,
your warmth lies beside me,
keeping me safe.
I couldn't have asked you to come into my life
at a more perfect time than you did.
It's as if my younger self saw me suffering,
and then sent me an angel.
You helped me heal,
and I will forever love you.

Benny - Sarah Pingel

I'm never going to be able to thank you enough.

I'm never going to love you hard enough.

There's not a thing I can do that would be enough to show you how grateful I am that you came into my life.

You mean every sunrise and every nightfall to me.

You mean every raindrop and every flower.

You mean more than every corner of this earth and every star in this galaxy.

I will never be able to explain to you how special you are to me.

I know now I needed you to help me learn how to love living.

I needed you to teach me to breathe again.

Thanks to B - Sarah Pingel

I'm outside breathing in the scent of the fresh morning air, the smell of dandelions and freshly cut grass passing by my nose. My hair is blowing around my face as I lay on a red and white checkered picnic blanket under a tall yet sturdy tree.

This is the happiness I longed for.

The happiness I dreamed for.

Summertime Joy - Sarah Pingel

I take for granted the way the wind in the summer makes my hair glide across my shoulders.

I take for granted the way it feels to walk through the creek with my bare feet as minnows swim over my toes.

I take for granted the way snow falls so elegantly on my tongue before it melts.

I take for granted the beating of my heart after I see something I love.

Depression makes me take for granted everything and dream of nothing.

But oh how I love the things life offers my soul, even if I sometimes take that for granted.

Life is Worth Loving - Sarah Pingel

I like the feeling of being absorbed by the earth.

Its moss growing over my skin,

Its water seeping into my veins.

I like the feeling of the sun as it shines through me until I am iridescent.

I like how I feel as I grow older with the earth,

both of us broken and yet both of us still aging as we try to erase the scars of the people who have hurt us.

I like how beautiful I feel as my body blends with the ground beneath my feet.

I look at the blue sky and blink my diamond eyes.

Thank you Mother Earth for this life I have,

no matter how hard it has been.

I continue to battle with the rain at times as it falls onto my head and seeps down my neck,

but I am no more at war with breathing in the fresh scent of living.

Peaceful Bliss - Sarah Pingel

I'm in my twenties now.

I still have depression,

I still have anxiety,

I still have so many things not going right in my life and in my head.

But I'm an adult.

I made it,

I really made it,

and I couldn't be more proud of myself for that.

Surviving the Inevitable - Sarah Pingel

I'm not sorry anymore for not being who you wanted me
to be.
This is who I am.
I'm anxious,
I'm shy,
I have episodes where it feels like my heart doesn't beat
for life anymore.
But I'm also happy,
I'm bright,
I'm loving,
I'm kind,
I'm strong.
I don't need your approval anymore.
I need my own.
I've always needed my own.
You could have grabbed my hand and led me to a sunnier
place.
You didn't have to leave me in the dark.
But I dug myself out as I continued to push towards the
sun.
I will now and forever fight to breathe in the sky.

I Am Me - Sarah Pingel

I've had a hard time looking at myself in the mirror,

at my body,

at my face.

I only saw what I didn't have,

and never what I did.

I wish I could have seen myself back then.

I wish I could have known I wasn't a failure for things I
couldn't control.

I wish the young girl who despised her body,

could see how confident she is now.

My Insecurities are my Beauties - Sarah Pingel

In this amount of beauty I finally feel,
I can't seem to think about my pain.
My heart aches,
my sorrow.
It's just gone.
Maybe only for an instant,
but it's an amazing instant and I love it.
I love it so much.

A Good Minute Feels like a Lifetime - Sarah Pingel

I like being naked.

Naked of clothing and normalities,

naked of the guilt people shed upon me.

I like how my boobs sulk and my hair lays against my shoulders.

The way my heart beats in my chest and my lips perch on my face.

I like being free of the life people think everyone needs to live.

I like being naked.

Bare Skin - Sarah Pingel

You realize who the most important people in your life are when your life gets at its worst.

You realize who actually cares about you when you stop caring about yourself.

You realize the meaning of happiness when you stop feeling it.

You realize the pain in your life when you can't bear to keep it anymore.

You never know what life is like,

how it's going to work out.

If it's going to end happily,

if it's going to end in a fountain of tears.

You never truly know how the world will work.

All you can really do is keep your head high,

find the right people,

and find yourself.

Realization - Sarah Pingel

I think I needed the pain you caused me in order to grow.

I didn't deserve it,

but I needed it to realize,

I'm more than a tool for others' enjoyment.

I'm Not a Universal Tool - Sarah Pingel

The sad thing is that I loved our friendship,

our sisterhood,

so much,

that I let it blind me to the fact that

you were never going to let yourself actually care for me.

So I grew,

I breathed,

and I learned that I am powerful,

even if you don't want to love me enough to see that.

Losing You to Find Me - Sarah Pingel

I sit and think about how you've affected me.

How it's not just your fault,

but mine too.

I always knew you would push me away eventually.

You never hid from the fact that you're a distant acquaintance,

that you don't let people get close because you're afraid to.

I always knew that about you,

I just couldn't stop myself from admiring your glimmer

or from becoming attached to you.

You never lied to me,

I just let myself believe that you would treat me different.

A fairytale of course.

But I am done blaming only you

for something I internally knew would happen.

Even if it hurts to admit that.

I Also Failed You - Sarah Pingel

Forgiving you is like sap dripping down my palm.

It's sticky, like the rumors that stayed in the mouths of strangers.

It's hard to remove, like the memory of your lies.

I scrub at it with anger and a hard head,

but if I would just stop struggling and lick it off with a healing heart,

it's sweeter and easier to clean away the agony you handed me.

Therapeutic Tree Sap - Sarah Pingel

I'm not mad at you anymore because,

at the time,

you felt just as crazy as I did.

The world felt like a box that was constantly getting

smaller for you,

just like it did for me.

Your lungs felt like they were filling with salt water every

second you breathed,

just like they did for me.

You were shushed and kicked until you couldn't stand

anymore,

and,

at the time,

I wasn't aware of that.

But now I can say wholeheartedly,

I am not mad at you anymore.

Forgiving the Past - Sarah Pingel

My soul eats at me when I'm angry.
When I'm mad at the world and at the people in it.
It hurts me to not pardon others actions,
but that doesn't make it any easier to forgive them.
Sometimes time and strength is all you need,
before being able to let yourself mend your heart.

I Need Time to Cope - Sarah Pingel

At some point in my life I let others tell me if I was worthy of being alive. I was just a teenager, a child, but I let others dictate how I felt about myself and how I looked at myself. I let the fear of being left out and companionless turn me into a person I didn't want to be. I became unkind in my own eyes, and it burns me to admit to that.

I wish I could take back how I acted the year I wanted to be accepted, but I can't and honestly, that's okay. I'm not that person anymore, she doesn't resonate with me in the slightest. I'm grown and I've learned from my mistakes. I will never be able to take back the pain I caused myself and the one I called my true friend, but I can say that I will never let myself turn into that person again. I will never have the need to be loved by all again. I will never have the need to please others at the cost of my humanity again. I will never hurt the ones who are purely mine again. I will forever hold myself accountable for the actions I caused during my declining year, but I'm finally letting go of the guilt I've carried for so long.

I will always wish for forgiveness and I will always have an ache in my heart, but I will not hold onto the little girl I was when I made those mistakes. I'm a woman now, and this woman right here, was carved from a completely different branch than the one all those years ago.

Girl Vs Women - Sarah Pingel

I hold my breasts in my hands.

They're soft and warm.

I look at them in all their natural beauty.

They're so lovely,

and they're all mine.

Self Made - Sarah Pingel

It's a new me staring back in the mirror.

Not the one that was touched without permission.

Not the one who was kissed even after no.

Not the one who was lied about.

Not the one that lost her friends.

Not the one who betrayed the ones she loved.

I'm a whole new me.

A healthier me,

a better me,

a happier me.

Forgetting You - Sarah Pingel

She hid within the stars for she thought the sun rejected
her.
But the sun did not pass her by,
it simply showed her there's more to life than shining
bright.

A Galaxy Full of Beginnings - Sarah Pingel

Dive in.

Accept the fact that sometimes the sun in your life is going to be covered by clouds

and it's going to be scary when the flowers you've been growing are drowned.

But it's also the most beautiful thing in the world when your light finally shines through the dark and your tulips finally blossom again.

The Patience of Believing in Yourself - Sarah Pingel

I'm thankful to be alive.

I'm thankful that I get to hear birds chirp in the morning.

I'm thankful that I can argue with my mom when we disagree about something:

I'm thankful that I get to laugh.

I'm thankful that I get to cry.

As much as life has pained me,

I'm thankful to breathe.

Thank You Lungs - Sarah Pingel

Let the feathers of hope grow across your brain.
Let the wings of strength guide your eyes.
Let the liftoff into the sky show you confidence.
Be like a bird,
happy and free.

Crow - Sarah Pingel

I realized that I'm not alone in this battle I have with my
heart and my mind.
I realized it when my sister had the same panic attacks as
I did.
I realized it when my best friend cried to me about the
pains she felt.
I realized it when a stranger said she was unloved and
broken.
The hurt I've felt my whole life runs through my veins the
same way it does someone else's.
Our situations may be different,
they may be the same,
but our blood runs through us like needles as we continue
to pick ourselves up day by day.
I am not alone in the suffering I've always felt.
As I write this,
someone's tears are dripping off their lips at the same time
mine are.
As I read this back,
someone's heart is mending slowly,
just like mine.

Healing is a Journey we all Share - Sarah Pingel

Sometimes I second guess happiness.

Like I'm not allowed to feel joy.

I feel as though any delights I have fill me with shame.

Shame of feeling anything but sad.

I think to myself,

am I really enjoying life right now?

Or am I just trying to make myself think I am?

But I deserve a great life,

I deserve true happiness.

And I will spend the rest of my life convincing my brain

that.

Never Ending - Sarah Pingel